Read all the books in the
Carlton Crumple Creature Catcher series:

Coming soon:

#2 Tater Invaders

Written and Illustrated by David Fremont

Color by Jimbo Matison

PIXEL✚INK

Text and illustrations copyright © 2020 by David Fremont
All rights reserved
Pixel+Ink is a division of Trustbridge Development Corp.
Printed and bound in February 2020 at Toppan Leefung, DongGuan City, China
Color by Jimbo Matison
Book design by Sammy Yuen
www.pixelandinkbooks.com
First Edition
1 3 5 7 9 10 8 6 4 2
Cataloging-in-Publication Data is available
from the Library of Congress

ISBN 978-1-645-95001-1 (hardcover)

For my beautiful creatures, with love:
Carol Tree Monkey, Milo Wolf,
and Greta Fox

CHAPTER 1

1

3

4

One day Carlton's older brother, Milt, got a brilliant, creepy older-brother-style idea...

Hey, I know, I'll dress up in horrible monster costumes and chase my younger brother, Carlton, around and he'll get scared and run away and cry and it will be SO AWESOME!

Oh no, Carlton, this is not something the cat coughed up. It's actual monster fur, yep!

And I MIGHT tell the monster not to eat you if you clean my room!!

OK! OK! Where's the vacuum?!

CHAPTER 2

Carlton began to fear everything.

He was afraid of what might be under the bed...

Down the hall...

...out in the yard...

Ahhhhhh!!!

16

Even in the kitchen...

Ahhhhh!!! Oh my garsh, what is THAT creature?!!

Little Carlton Crumple believed monsters were everywhere.

So Carlton told his little next-door-neighbor pal, Lulu.

They're coming, Lulu! The monsters are coming, I tell you! They're around every corner! Waiting to grab us! Oh, the humanity!!!

Lulu just rolled her eyes.

Huh? What do you mean, Lulu?

OK already. The monsters are coming. I guess we're doomed. Now what?

We're doomed! Unless some skilled creature-catcher dude steps forward, which I don't think is gonna happen anytime soon because I don't think that dude even exists!

Yep. No such thing as a creature catcher and there never will be. Oh well. Doomed, doomed, doomed.

Oh my garsh, he doesn't exist? That's terrible!

Then Carlton had an epiphany, which is like a great idea that you've been waiting for your whole life that suddenly explodes inside your head.

Of course, it's up to me!
I've got to do it! I can't live my whole
life running! I'm turning the tables!
Right here, right now!

CHAPTER 3

But the monsters that once chased Carlton around suddenly stopped showing up. Coincidentally, it was about the same time that Milt lost interest in scaring Carlton and became obsessed with watching *Big Trux* on TV. But Carlton knew unseen horrors could be waiting around any corner.

So he continued honing his creature-catching skills. He watched and studied late-night Creature Features movies. And read stacks of horror comics.

He tried out attack drills on the family...
like his mom, for instance...

HI-YAH!!!

AHHHHH!!

27

But Carlton's dad finally had enough. So after enduring Carlton's ridiculous creature-catching shenanigans, he told his son:

Carlton Crumple, you need to forget about all this ridiculous creature-catching stuff! You need a job!!

Carlton thought it wasn't a bad idea. Then he could save up his money to buy creature-catching gear, gizmos, helmet, body armor, and awesome stuff!

So eleven-year-old Carlton enrolled in a special youth work-training program at the local fast-food restaurant Chubbzy Cheeseburgers...

But even while on the job, Carlton continued to practice his skills...

...Carlton-Crumple, Creature Catcher!

CHAPTER 4

MEANWHILE...A few miles up the road, modern society was about to collapse. And it all started with a french fry.

That's right. Some silly little kid was sitting on the beach eating a Laffy Daffy Lunch Meal from Chubbzy Cheeseburgers, the number-one fast-food restaurant in the world (1.5 gazillion sold, quite frankly).

The french fry floated away and then it sank to the bottom of the lake.

But the tantalizing smell of the french fry awakened a very large, ancient lake creature that had taken up residence beneath a rock. It had been hibernating there for a thousand years, because everyone knows that's what lake creatures do until something suddenly awakens them. Suffice it to say, the french fry was that something.

The creature gobbled the french fry down in one gulp. It was the most amazing thing it had ever tasted (plus it hadn't eaten anything in a really, really, really long time). So it woke up its ancient-lake-creature family and informed them in creature-speak that they must journey forth and find more of this food!

It led them to the beach. Luckily, all the people had long since left, but that darned little kid had left the remainder of his Laffy Daffy Lunch Meal.

Oh, way to go, little kid!

The creatures went wild and gobbled it down, including the free toy prize inside. But that wasn't enough. They were still hungry. They needed MORE!

After scaring some stinky, hairy hippies out of their van, the even stinkier, hairier lake creatures hopped in and headed down the highway in search of more delicious fast food.

40

Luckily for the creatures, the highway had lots of Chubbzy Cheeseburgers signs. So the creatures just followed them. There was a Chubbzy sign about every ten feet.

43

CHAPTER 5

MEANWHILE...up the highway a few miles at a Chubbzy Cheeseburgers restaurant...

And the next time you decide to put chili sauce on a burger instead of ketchup, you're FIRED!

...mild-mannered fast-food worker Carlton Crumple was being reprimanded by his boss, Manager Floops...

Then the hungry creatures entered the restaurant. No one paid much attention to the "hairy hippies" that had come out of the van.

49

But Carlton knew something was weird about them when they ordered two hundred Laffy Daffy Lunch Meals and swallowed them whole without even taking the food out of the bag.

So Carlton informed Manager Floops of the impending danger.

CHAPTER 6

And then Carlton and his faithful sidekick, Lulu, her "attack poodle" Poof-Poof and Poof-Poof's best pal Iggy the Iguana all jumped onto Lulu's motorized scooter and hit the highway in hot pursuit of the terrible and horrific Munchies! All they had to do was follow the Chubbzy Cheeseburgers signs and the crumpled burger wrappers!!!

This is all too exciting! Let's take a commercial break, folks...

Do you like deep-fried, mouthwatering buckets of fudge-dunked cheese chunks slathered in bacon bits then triple-dipped in hot caramel product, then rolled in powdered sugar and smothered in hot pancake syrup all squished between a hamburger bun...?? Well, DO YA?!?

Then get yer big ol' fat butt on in to Chubbzy Cheeseburgers where—

59

CHAPTER 7

The cross-country chase was on to GET THE MUNCHIES! Cops! Nerds! Hippies! Monsters! Poodles! Cheeseburgers! Awesome!

Then the Munchie leader suddenly spit something out of his mouth onto the side of the road!

PA-TOOOIE!!!

Aw, sick! What the heck is
that disgusting blob?!!

SPLAT!

66

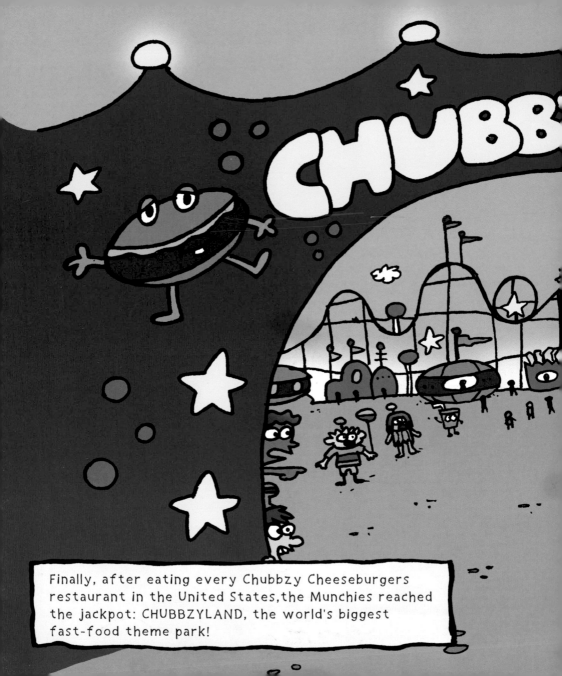

Finally, after eating every Chubbzy Cheeseburgers restaurant in the United States, the Munchies reached the jackpot: CHUBBZYLAND, the world's biggest fast-food theme park!

CHAPTER 8

75

77

81

Carlton used everything he had. He shot at the Munchies with his Spatula Crossbow!

He tried to blind them with his Hot Mustard Squirter!

He even flung his Frozen 100% Mostly Beef Patty Ninja Stars at them!

But it was no use. The Munchies just stood there as Carlton's stealth ammo bounced off them. Then they proceeded toward the delicious Cheeseburger Train to chow down!

CHAPTER 9

So the Munchie swallowed Carlton Crumple in one gulp.

GLORP!

SPLUT!

TRANSLATION: "YUM! YUM!"

CHAPTER 10

94

The horrible and terrifying Munchies went back to sleep for another thousand years. Unless, of course, one of them decides to wake up for a midnight snack or, like, another silly kid throws a french fry into the lake or something crazy like that.

CHAPTER 11

Back at Chubbzyland, everyone cheered Carlton Crumple for saving humanity. Lulu gave him another high five. He turned redder than chili sauce.

CARLTON CRUMPLE
CREATURE CATCHER!!!

Meanwhile...

Well that was dee-lish! Nothing like *splitting* a Laffy Daffy Meal after an exciting adventure, right, Iggy?

107

Carlton Crumple
Creature Catcher Book 2:
Tater Invaders

Carlton Crumple will do battle with
horrifying underground potato creatures!
Oh my garsh, grab the ketchup!

ABOUT THE AUTHOR

DAVID FREMONT grew up in Fremont, California—yep, a Fremont from Fremont! He loved watching *Underdog* cartoons, reading comics, and drawing with his brother. When David was eleven, his cousin Steve showed him a super-cool shark comic that he had drawn, inspiring David to start drawing his own comics. When David grew up, he moved across the bay to San Francisco, where he got a job painting cartoons at an animation studio. While at Colossal Pictures, he created projects for Cartoon Network and Disney. More recently, after moving to Los Angeles, he created a pilot for Nickelodeon and an online kids series for DreamWorksTV, called *Public Pool*. He currently lives in Woodland Hills, with his family (and many furry pet creatures!), where he teaches cartooning classes to kids. This is his first book for children.

ACKNOWLEDGMENTS

Double cheeseburgers to all who helped get the Munchies out into the world and make my comic book dreams a reality: Editor-in-chief Bethany Buck for being a believer in Carlton Crumple; Kyra Reppen and all the kind folks at Pixel+Ink, Trustbridge Global Media, and Holiday House; cartoon champion Mary Harrington at Nickelodeon; color rock-star rescuer pal Jimbo Matison; design wizard Sammy Yuen; and legal hero LeighAnna MacFadden. Chili sauce to my author/illustrator friend James Proimos for encouraging me to write and illustrate a book. Super-size fries to my i3 artist friends Eric White and Brad Mossman for lifelong friendship and inspiration. A side of hash browns to Jan Johns for her creature-voiced pep talks. Quesadillas to my siblings Nancy, Lisa, Diane, and Mark for all the homemade munchies, late-night Creature Features, and family road trips that fueled this book. An ice cream sundae with whipped cream on top to my sweet Mom for enrolling me in summertime cartooning classes, and a big baked potato with Salad Supreme to my Dad for telling me to never give up and to "get it done!" Finally, Laffy Daffy meal prizes to my wife, Carol, and children, Milo and Greta, for all their support, love, and laughter.